For my family: James, Bethany, and Matthew
I'd run through forests for each of you.
I love you!—J.H.L.

For Sei and Sena
Thank you for remembering me.
—G.W.B.

ISBN 978-0-9851005-2-0

Printed in China

LazyOne, Inc.
Timbuktu, Madagascar, Bronx,
Fargo, Little Rock, Tijuana, Siberia.

THIS BOOK BELONGS TO:

Name: _____

Phone: _____

LAZY one®

Duck Duck Moose

By Jennifer H. Lyman

Illustrated by Gideon Burnett

One spring morning, a family of ducks took a waddle by the river. They wanted some breakfast.

But while looking for berries, they found a surprise! A baby moose was nestled in the bulrushes.

The baby moose opened his left eye.
He opened his right eye.
He took a good, long look at the ducks.
Then he opened his mouth and said…

MAMA!

And from that moment on,
the duck family included one shaggy brown moose.

Moose loved his family.
They taught him how to quack!

QUAHHH!

They taught him how to waddle—back and forth, back and forth.

And they taught him how to dive in the pond for fish eggs and algae.

All spring and summer,
they played in the wetlands.
They sang "moose-ical" numbers.

HIGH
SCHOOL
MOOSE-ICAL

They wrote silly "moose-ages" in the riverbank.

And they spent many hours playing
their favorite games: *Goosie Says, Mallard May I...*

...and *Red Rover*.

Then one day, the wind turned cold. Crunchy, golden leaves fell from the trees, right onto Moose's antlers.
Autumn had arrived.

It was time for the duck family to fly south for the winter.
But they had a BIG problem—Moose couldn't fly.

So they came up with a terrific plan: the ducks would fly, and Moose would walk, following below them.

Well, it turns out that ducks can fly *much* faster than a moose can walk.

Soon, Moose had to jog to keep up with his family.

And *then* he had to
full-out sprint
just to keep them in sight!

Then he had to run.

Friendly animals tried to talk to Moose as he ran, but he wouldn't stop. He'd just say,

Quackity quack quack!

and keep on running!

Birdwatchers, hunters, and zoologists soon noticed the sprinting moose. What a sight! They launched studies and wrote papers and held symposiums.

Squirrels, ferrets, and other woodland critters dropped in
to hitch a ride on Moose's antlers as he ran.
(Moose didn't seem to mind.)

It wasn't long before the national media learned about the duck-chasing moose.
They even put a picture of Moose on the 10:00 news!

Day in and day out, Moose kept up with his family.

And as he ran, he got warmer and warmer.

Finally, he arrived in the balmy south.

The duck family was so happy to be together again!
They quacked and waddled and flapped.
Then they threw a big party!

Everyone enjoyed Moose's favorite dessert.

And the ducks all gave Moose a nice, relaxing "moosage" to soothe all his aches and pains.

And children everywhere, inspired by Moose's famous, duck-chasing journey, started playing a brand-new party game.
Maybe you've heard of it?

Duck…
        Duck…
                Moose!